CLAUDE

ADVENTURES

THREE STORIES IN ONE

In the Spotlight
Lights! Camera! Action!
Going for Gold

Alex T. Smith

h HODDER

HODDER CHILDREN'S BOOKS
Claude in the Spotlight first published in Great Britain in 2013
by Hodder and Stoughton
Claude Lights! Camera! Action! and *Claude Going for Gold* first published
in Great Britain in 2016 by Hodder and Stoughton
This edition first published in 2018 by Hodder and Stoughton

1 3 5 7 9 10 8 6 4 2

Text and illustrations copyright © Alex T. Smith, 2013, 2016
The moral rights of the author have been asserted.

A CIP catalogue record for this book is available from the British Library.

ISBN: 978 1 444 94670 3

Design by Alison Still

Printed and bound in China

The paper and board used in this book are made from wood from
responsible sources.

MIX
Paper from
responsible sources
FSC
www.fsc.org FSC® C104740

Hodder Children's Books
An imprint of Hachette Children's Group
Carmelite House, 50 Victoria Embankment, London EC4Y 0DZ
An Hachette UK Company
www.hachettechildrens.co.uk
www.hachette.co.uk

CLAUDE

in the Spotlight

Behind a red front door with
a big brass knocker, lives a
little dog named Claude.

And here he is!

hello!

4

Fancy red beret

stylish red sweater

well polished shoes

Claude is a small dog.
Claude is a small, plump dog.
Claude is a small, plump dog
who wears a fancy red beret
and a stylish red sweater.

Claude's owners are Mr and Mrs Shinyshoes and his best friend is Sir Bobblysock.

Sir Bobblysock is both a sock and quite bobbly.

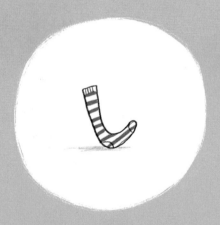

Every morning, Mr and Mrs
Shinyshoes wave goodbye to Claude
and set off for work. And that is
when the fun begins. Where will
Claude and Sir Bobblysock go today?

One day, shortly after Mr and Mrs Shinyshoes had skedaddled out of the door, Claude leapt out of bed with a spring in his step, dislodging Sir Bobblysock's hairnet and almost knocking over his cup of tea.

Claude should have been feeling rather sleepy because the night before he had stayed up VERY late (until about half past eight) reading a book of ghost stories.

Some of the ghosts were very spooky looking. Claude was especially worried about how they floated about and didn't wear any shoes...

11

But that was last night.
Now Claude was wide-awake
with his beret on, looking for
something to do.

'I think I will go for a walk
into town,' he said, so he did.

Sir Bobblysock decided to go too. Really his hair wanted washing, but he felt that no good would come of him lounging about all day with his head wrapped up in a towel, so the two friends set off.

THEATRE

This Afternoon Only!

The **VARIETY SHOW**

AMAZING ACTS! DARING FEATS!
WORLD FAMOUS PERFORMERS!
AND A SPECIAL
GRAND PRIZE!

Suddenly, a troupe of
children walked by.

They seemed to be wearing
some very funny outfits.
Very funny indeed…

Claude's nose tingled, his eyebrows wiggled, and behind him his bottom started to wag his tail. There was DEFINITELY an adventure brewing here!

Quickly smoothing down his ears, Claude ran after the children with Sir Bobblysock hopping along behind.

They followed the children
into a big, bright room. The
wall on one side was completely
covered by a mirror. There was
a tall upright piano in one corner
and an old lady sitting
at it, playing a very jolly tune.

Claude was just about to ask if
he could play a little ditty, when
the classroom door flew open.

Into the room leapt an extraordinary looking woman!

'Good morning, everybody!' the lady boomed. 'My name is Miss Henrietta Highkick-Spin, and I'm your teacher. Now come along, everyone, let's daaaaance!'

It all looked a bit too much for Sir Bobblysock who had his knees to consider, so he went and lay on the top of the piano.

'First,' called Miss Highkick-Spin,
'we must warm up our bodies!'
and she began skipping about and
doing all sorts of strange stretches.

Claude found the skipping very
easy indeed and he enjoyed the
breeze around his ears as he
        galloped across the room.

The stretches, however, were
a different matter.

Claude found that his
tummy got in the way…

After everyone was nice and warm,
Miss Highkick-Spin taught the
class a nice gentle dance routine.

There was some more skipping about, some leg waggling, and some 'waving-your-arms-above-your-head-and-pretending-you-are-a-daisy-in-a-windy-meadow'.

Claude tried really hard to join in, but when it came to the arm waving his paws got knotted in his ears.

'Don't worry,' said Miss Highkick-Spin, 'Ballet's not for everyone. Let's try some tap!' And she handed Claude some exciting new shoes.

Claude put them on and thought he looked lovely. When he walked they made a wonderful TAP TAP TAP noise on the floor. He showed them to Sir Bobblysock who said they were great, but that he felt one of his heads coming on.

Miss Highkick-Spin
was just about to
teach the class a noisy
new dance when
something happened...

A tiny fly, who had seen Claude waving his arms above his head and pretending to be a daisy in a windy meadow...

...went up Claude's jumper!

Claude couldn't help himself.
It tickled.

He skittered
and jittered
across the room.

He leapt
and dived
high up
into the air.

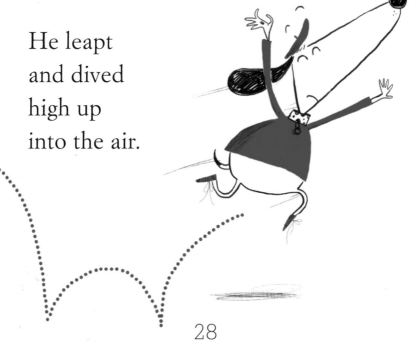

28

He wiggled and
jiggled all over until
he was almost a blur.

Sir Bobblysock
needed a big cup
of tea from just
looking at him.

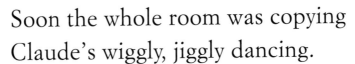

Soon the whole room was copying
Claude's wiggly, jiggly dancing.
Even the old lady joined in
with the leg kicking and
bottom shaking!

30

Eventually the fly got a bit
bored, escaped from
Claude's jumper and
disappeared out of
the window.

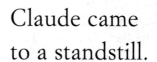

Claude came
to a standstill.

'Phew!' panted the dance teacher, pink in the face. 'What a wonderful new dance! You MUST join us in the show we are performing in at the theatre this afternoon! Do say you will?'

Claude didn't like to ask what a theatre was, so he just smoothed his jumper over his tummy and nodded politely.

About an hour later, after the children had eaten their packed lunches and Claude and Sir Bobblysock had tucked into the emergency picnic that Claude always kept under his beret, the whole class set off for the theatre.

THEATRE

This Afternoon Only!
The
VARIETY
SHOW
AMAZING ACTS! DARING FEATS!
WORLD FAMOUS PERFORMERS!
AND A SPECIAL
GRAND PRIZE!

On the way, one of the girls explained to Claude all about the show they would soon be starring in. It was going to be a variety show.

'That means lots of different people do different things on the stage,' said the girl. 'We will be doing your new dance! And the most exciting thing is that today, the best act wins a grand prize – all the cakes you can eat from Mr Lovelybuns' Bakery. He's judging the competition.'

Claude clapped his paws together
and Sir Bobblysock let out a sigh.

Mr Lovelybuns' Bakery was Claude's favourite shop. Even Sir Bobblysock, who could be quite picky with his pastries, had declared that Mr Lovelybuns had the nicest buns he'd ever seen.

Unfortunately, in
the excitement,
nobody saw a
suspicious looking
man listening in on
their conversation...

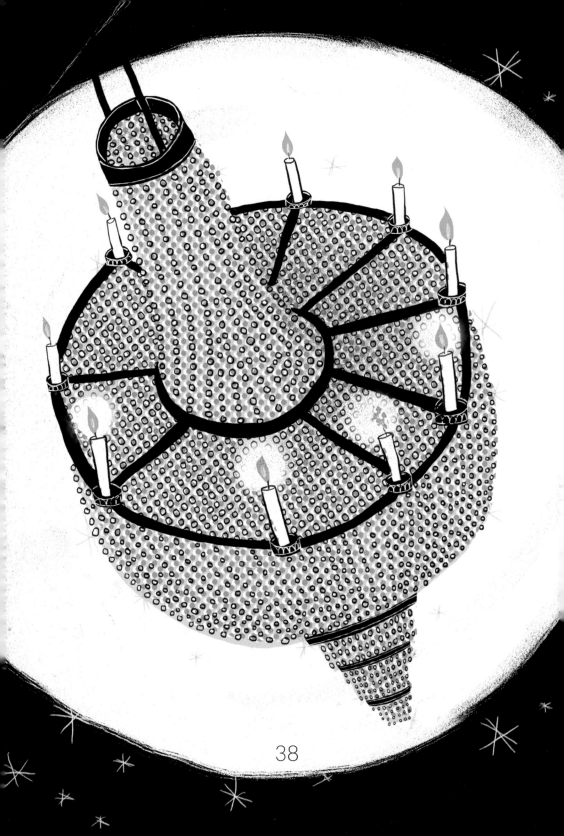

Claude and Sir Bobblysock
liked the theatre immediately.
Sir Bobblysock liked the
glitz and glamour of the
whole place.

High above the audience's
seats was a big, sparkly
chandelier. Sir Bobblysock
said that you wouldn't want
that falling on your head.
Claude nodded his head in
agreement, then everyone
trouped off backstage.

Claude couldn't believe how different it was. It was dark and dusty and rather spooky.

'This is just the sort of place a ghost would live,' shivered Claude, remembering his book of ghosties at home.

HAS ANYONE
SEEN MY
TROUSERS?
*THE CLASSIC
TRAGEDY*

starring Sidney Thomas

★ ★ ★ ★ ★

BILLY BONGO
in
Who's
Afraid of
Virginia Woof?

★ ★ ★ ★ ★   ★ ★ ★ ★ ★

Harriet J. Harmon
in
THE SMASH HIT
★Hello★
SAILORS!

✦ ✦ ✦ ✦ ✦

THE INTERNATIONALLY
ACCLAIMED MUSICAL

PUSSYCATS
starring Corinne Gotch

LIMITED RUN! BOOK NOW!

1.

THE DANCING
DIVA'S
DANCE
TROUPE

And he and Sir
Bobblysock quickly
hurried along to
the brightly lit
dressing rooms.

In the first room they found a
troupe of ladies who would be
doing a dance routine, too. Sir
Bobblysock couldn't take his eyes
off the ladies' extraordinary costumes.

In the next room was The Marvellous Marvin, a magician.

Claude and Sir Bobblysock watched in amazement as he waggled his magic wand about and produced three tiny rabbits from his hat.

44

Then Claude had a go…

In the final dressing room was an enormous woman dressed as a viking.

Her special trick was singing –
so high and so loud that she could
shatter a teacup. Claude and Sir
Bobblysock put on the safety
goggles that Claude
always kept under his beret
and watched as the viking
demonstrated with her teacup.

AAAAAA!!!

Claude was very impressed.
Sir Bobblysock just pursed his
lips. What a way to treat a teacup!

49

Of course, Claude couldn't wait to
have a go, but as hard as he tried,
the glass vase wouldn't budge.

Eventually Sir Bobblysock slyly
elbowed it off the table...

Claude was just enjoying a pre-show
biscuit when there came a shout
from down the corridor...

The Marvellous
Marvin was
standing in front
of the dressing
room looking
very pale.

52

'A g-g-g-ghost just jumped out at me and tried to snatch my magic wand,' he said shakily. 'It's broken, look!'

He held up the wand. It was all bent and limp like a sad sock.

'The Theatre Ghost!' said Miss. Highkick-Spin dramatically. 'Every theatre has a ghost, but I've never heard of one behaving so badly before.'

Claude shivered. He would
have to keep his eyes peeled for
this ghost. It was clearly trouble
with a capital T. Sir Bobblysock
couldn't stop his bobbles from
shaking. All this talk of ghosts
had given him the collywobbles.

Before anyone could say any
more, a man with a clipboard
bustled through the crowd.

'Places please, everyone!' he said.
'The show is about to begin!'

Claude and Sir Bobblysock rushed
to the side of the stage to watch.

But first, they couldn't help
popping their heads through
the plush red curtains to
look at the audience.

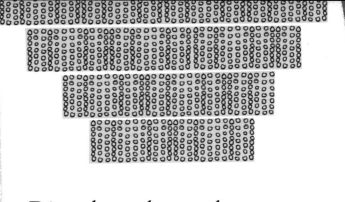

Directly underneath
the big chandelier
was Mr Lovelybuns.

He was sitting at a special judging table and looked very important. Claude waved and Mr Lovelybuns waved back.

Suddenly the orchestra started up and the show began.

The dancing ladies were
halfway through their hot shoe
shuffle when the ghost leapt
out from the darkness and
terrified them. One by one,
they all fell over.

The last dancer tumbled head first into the orchestra pit and got her head stuck in a tuba.

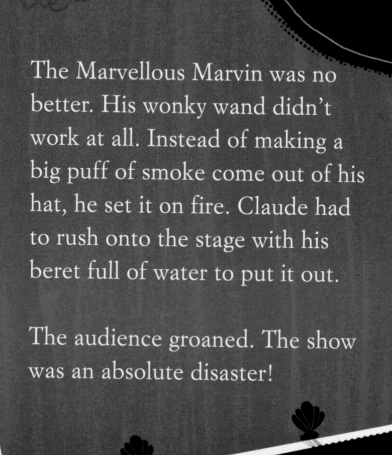

The Marvellous Marvin was no better. His wonky wand didn't work at all. Instead of making a big puff of smoke come out of his hat, he set it on fire. Claude had to rush onto the stage with his beret full of water to put it out.

The audience groaned. The show was an absolute disaster!

Soon it was
Claude's turn to
take to the stage.
Sir Bobblysock
watched from
the wings.

Claude shuffled on
with the other dancers
and when the music
started, he nervously
wiggled and jiggled about.

All of a sudden, Claude heard the stomping of shoes behind him.

He spun around on the spot and there was the ghost!

Miss Highkick-Spin screamed. The children squealed and everyone hotfooted it into the wings.

Claude joined Sir Bobblysock backstage and Sir Bobblysock hid up Claude's jumper. He was all of a quiver and desperately needed one of his long lie downs.

'Something isn't quite right here,' thought Claude, and he thought so hard that his head started to hurt.

The viking was the next act. She had already smashed a tumbler and a crystal statue of a poodle when Claude saw the ghost tiptoe onto the stage behind her.

Claude looked
at the ghost – from the top of its
white head to the bottom of its shoes.

SHOES!

70

That was it!
Claude wagged
his tail. None of the ghosts in
his book at home wore shoes –
especially not great galumphing
ones like that. They floated
daintily about, shoeless.

So if this ghost was wearing shoes,
it couldn't be a real ghost at all.

72

Claude ran onto the stage.

'This isn't a ghostie!' he cried.
'It is a very naughty person indeed.'

And he grabbed the ghost's
white sheet and pulled it off.
Underneath was a shifty-
looking man. His face
was very red and he
looked down at
the floor.

Everybody gasped
like this: GASP!

'What on earth are you up to, you naughty man?' said Claude

Sir Bobblysock hopped out from Claude's jumper and put his specs on so he could get a better look at the action.

'I just LOVE cakes,' said the
naughty man, 'and when I heard
someone telling you that the grand
prize was all the cakes you could eat,
I wanted to win them. Only, I'm not
very good at anything…'

The audience said 'Aaaaaaaaah' sadly.

'So I thought if could stop everyone else from winning, I could come on and do anything and win the competition...'

The audience said 'Oooooooh' crossly.

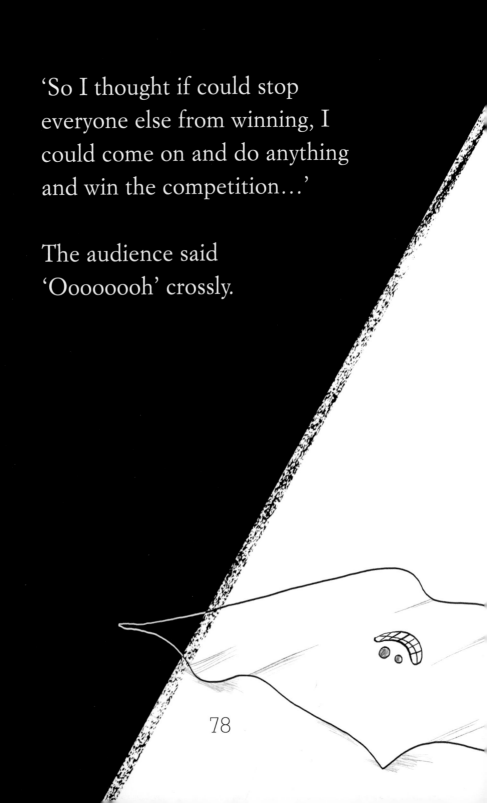

'So I went to Ida Down's Bed Emporium and bought myself this sheet and...'

Claude was just going to wag his finger at the naughty man, when –

Mr Lovelybuns let out a yelp!
The big chandelier above his
head looked like it was about to
fall. The viking's scream must
have set it off. If Mr Lovelybuns
didn't move, the whole
thing would crash
down on his head!

Everybody watched as the
chandelier swayed. Then all
of a sudden it started to fall!

Everyone panicked.
Everyone except Claude.

'Quick!' cried Claude to the naughty man and they ran over to Mr Lovelybuns.

Sir Bobblysock had a dizzy fit and fell over with a swoon.

Claude and the naughty man stretched out the ghost's white sheet just in time and...

...caught the chandelier!

'Bravo!' said Mr Lovelybuns, clambering out from his seat. 'Claude, you saved the day. YOU are the winner of the competition!'

Everybody in the theatre clapped and some even threw flowers. Claude blushed and shyly shook Mr Lovelybuns' hand. Sir Bobbysock moved to the side on account of his hay fever.

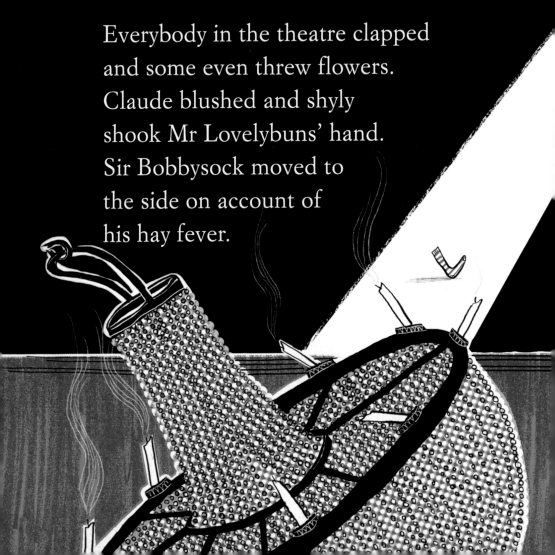

Miss Highkick-Spin fought
her way through the crowds.

'Claude,' she said, with tears
in her eyes. 'You are the most
wonderful dancer I've ever seen.
Won't you and Sir Bobblysock
come and travel the world with
me and dance in theatres all
over the place?'

Claude thought about
it for a moment.

Now that he'd got the hang of it,
he did rather enjoy dancing and
shaking his bottom about. But
then he did love
         living at Mr and Mrs
         Shinyshoes' house too.

He looked at Sir Bobblysock.
He was as white as a sheet
and looked like he had seen a
hundred ghosts.

What he needed was one of his
long lie downs with a cup of tea
and a cream horn.

Claude politely explained all
of this to Miss Highkick-Spin
who understood.

Then, after saying goodbye
to everyone, Claude and Sir
Bobblysock made their way
home, only stopping to call
into Mr Lovelybuns' Bakery.

Later that day, when Mr and Mrs Shinyshoes came home from work, they were surprised to find their kitchen full of cakes and pastries.

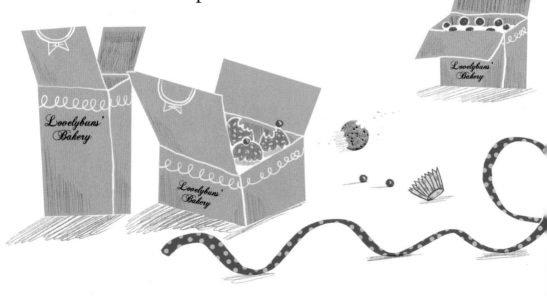

'Where on earth have all these cakes come from?' said Mrs Shinyshoes. 'Do you think Claude knows anything about them?'

Mr Shinyshoes laughed. 'Don't be silly – look, he's been fast asleep all day!'

But of course Claude
DID know where all the
cakes had come from.

And we do too, don't we?

CLAUDE

Lights! Camera! Action!

In a house on Waggy Avenue,
number 112 to be exact, there
lives a dog called CLAUDE.

Claude is a dog.
Claude is a small dog.
Claude is a small, plump dog
who wears the snazziest of
sweaters and a jaunty red beret.

jaunty red beret

snazzy sweater

Claude lives with his best friend Sir Bobblysock who is both a sock and quite bobbly.

He also lives with Mr and Mrs Shinyshoes.

Every day Claude waits for them
to shout 'Cheerio!' and skip out
of the door to work, then he and
Sir Bobblysock have an adventure.

Where will our two chums go
today...?

One morning (it was a Thursday) Claude was in the garden with his beret on, and he was being VERY busy and important.

Sir Bobblysock was out there too – lying on a sun lounger with his cardigan around his shoulders.

It was the first time he'd been out
of the house for a week, as he'd
had a chill all down the one side.

Claude was busily and
importantly hanging out all his
dressing-up costumes to dry.

'There!' he said, stepping back to admire his handiwork. 'Now it is time for a treat!'

Claude whipped his beret off and had a jolly good rummage around until he found what he was looking for – a gigantic box with a trampoline inside.

It had arrived in the post the other day – a present from one of Claude's friends who had a circus.

Claude set up the trampoline and started to bounce.

Up and down Claude went, high up in the air. His ears flapped about beautifully behind him.

'Come and have a go!' Claude called to Sir Bobblysock.

Sir Bobblysock said that he'd love to, but he'd just had a cream horn and didn't want it coming back up again with all the bobbling about.

Claude continued to bounce. The higher he got, the more he could see of Waggy Avenue.

There was Miss Highkick-Spin jazz-stepping her way to the dance studio.

And there was
Mr Lovelybuns
titivating his
buns as usual.

And there was a giant
gorilla in a dressing gown,
drinking a cup of tea.

A GORILLA??

IN A DRESSING
GOWN??

DRINKING
A CUP OF TEA??

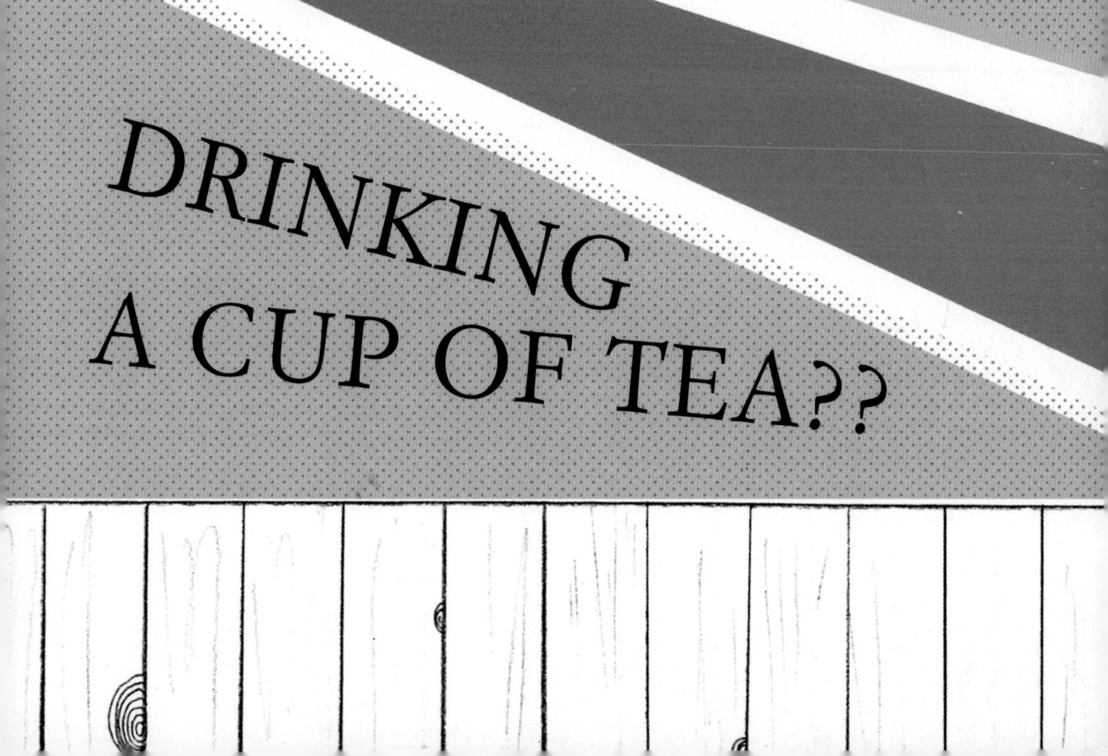

What on earth was a giant gorilla doing on Waggy Avenue?

Claude's eyebrows started to waggle. His bottom started to wobble, and his tail began to wag so fast it was a blur.

Quickly Claude stopped bouncing and stashed the trampoline back in his beret.

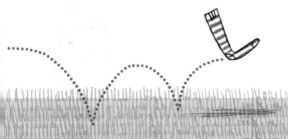

'I am going to investigate this gorilla!' he cried, and ran off with Sir Bobblysock bouncing along behind him.

Unfortunately, in his excitement to find out what was going on, Claude managed to get his foot caught in a dangly bit of the washing line and – TWAAAANNNNGGGGG! – the whole thing fell down.

'Oh bother!' he said and quickly stuffed all his costumes back in his beret without even taking them off the line.

Then Claude and Sir Bobblysock went through the front door, down the steps, and out into Waggy Avenue.

Cor! There was ever such a
lot to look at! Claude had
never seen Waggy Avenue
looking quite like this before.

IBRARY

Mr Lovelybuns Bakery
The Best Buns in Town!

Curl Up
and Dye
Hair & Beauty

BROWN
TO EARTH
Electricals & Lighting

AT MY
WICK'S END
scented candles

HEAVY PETAL
Florist

Everywhere he and Sir Bobblysock looked there were gigantic spotlights, whirring cameras and big fluffy microphones poking here, there and everywhere.

LANET of the RAPES

Miss Reed's
READ-A-LOT
BOOKSHOP
WE LIKE BIG BOOKS
AND WE CANNOT LIE

Miss Melons'
LOVELY PEAR
Fruit and Vegetable
Emporium

IDA DOWN'S
edsheet emporium

ALL SHOOK UP!
· milkshakes · hotdogs · burgers ·

Claude was just ogling at
it all when he tripped over
a bit of washing line that
had escaped from his beret.
Three somersaults later, he
landed SMACK BANG in
front of one of the waggling
film cameras!

He was just thinking what
a splendid landing that was
– bent knees, no wobble,
GORGEOUS smile – when
someone shouted 'CUT!' and
marched over to Claude. He
looked very frowny despite the
fact that he was also wearing a
snazzy hat, which was currently
at the jauntiest of angles.

'What are you doing!?' cried the man. 'Can't you see that we are in the middle of making a film? You just tumbled into our shot!'

Claude quickly stuffed the dangly bit of washing line back under his beret, smoothed his jumper down over his tummy and said 'sorry' in his nicest voice. This seemed to make the man with the megaphone much happier.

'It's OK,' he said, 'it was only a rehearsal. My name is Everard Zoom-Lens, and I am directing this film called Gorilla Thriller! It stars these two actors here – Errol Heart-Throb and Gloria Swoon.'

Claude introduced himself and Sir Bobblysock. Claude told Gloria Swoon that he liked her dangly earrings. Sir Bobblysock went a bit pink when Errol Heart-Throb shook his hand, and felt ever so glad he'd put his curlers in the night before.

'And this is our wonderful gorilla,'
said Everard. 'His name is Alan.'

The enormous gorilla
stood up and gave
Claude and Sir
Bobblysock a
very dramatic bow.

He'd been
classically trained.

'Would you like to watch us make our film?' asked Gloria.

Claude had never seen a film being made before so said, 'Yes please!' in his Outdoor Voice. Sir Bobblysock had seen one before, years ago, but that's a different story.

'You can sit yourself down there,' said Everard Zoom-Lens, 'and watch. There's lots for us to do before we can start filming properly.'

So Claude and Sir Bobblysock settled themselves down and watched closely as Errol Heart-Throb, Gloria Swoon and the gorilla rehearsed their scene.

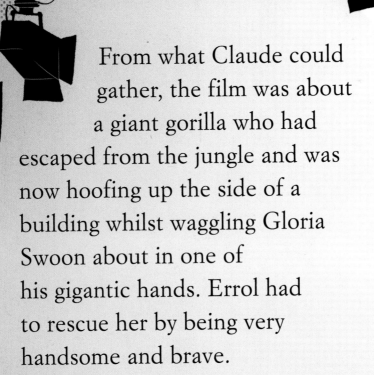

From what Claude could gather, the film was about a giant gorilla who had escaped from the jungle and was now hoofing up the side of a building whilst waggling Gloria Swoon about in one of his gigantic hands. Errol had to rescue her by being very handsome and brave.

It was terribly exciting.

'Right!' said Everard eventually.
'Everyone take five!'

Everyone shuffled off to their
trailers to prepare for the
afternoon's filming, leaving
Claude and Sir Bobblysock alone.

First, Claude sat on his seat
and slurped a juice carton.
Sir Bobblysock nibbled a fig roll.

Then Claude swung his
legs for a bit and sighed.

Sitting down and waiting
was awfully boring
sometimes.

Soon, Claude's eyes started
to wander...

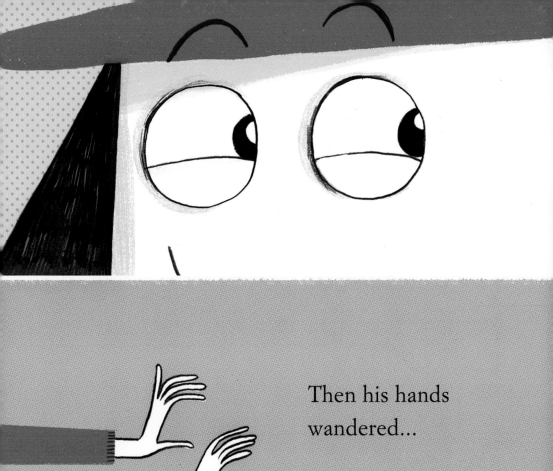

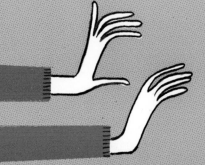

Then his hands wandered...

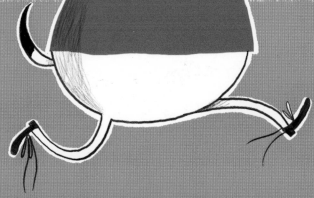

...and finally his legs followed too.

He was just sneaking back to his
seat after some terrific snooping
when a bit of the washing line
escaped from under his hat again.

'This is going to cause a terrific accident,' he said. Claude tried to stuff it back under his beret but it managed to wrap itself around one of his feet and...

Yowzer!

This time, Claude's landing wasn't anywhere near as splendid.

136

But at least his bottom had found something soft to bump onto...

...a **big**

box of wigs!

FILM: GORILLA
THRILLER!

.WIGS.

Wigs, Claude discovered, were hairstyles that weren't attached to heads, which meant that you could try as many on as you wanted...

Claude thought he looked lovely with a full head of soft waves.

Sir Bobblysock decided to keep it all very casual.

'There you are!' said Everard Zoom-Lens. 'And you've found the wigs! Goodo! Would you be so kind as to help get them on the actors so we can start filming?'

The two chums helped the actors put on their wigs. They did it VERY busily and VERY importantly.

Errol Heart-Throb had one with a kiss curl. He also had quite a ravishing fake moustache.

Gloria Swoon wore a blonde wig full of bouncy curls.

Alan had a terribly stylish toupee.

The next thing that needed to
be done was make-up.

'We need them to look
beautiful and very
glamorous!' said Everard
through his megaphone.

Claude thought faces weren't THAT different from colouring-in books. He also had some felt-tip pens, an emergency glue stick and some glitter in his beret.

As Everard dashed off to tell someone where they could put their bananas, Claude set to work...

The effect was rather striking.

'Er-lovely,' said Everard,
not quite as excitedly as
Claude had hoped. 'Let's get
into costumes and
get this film started...'

All the actors and Alan
bustled off to their trailers
to get changed.

When they emerged again, they looked like different people.

Claude clapped his paws together and Sir Bobblysock went a bit giddy at the sight of Gloria's sequins.

'Places please!' cried Everard, and everyone hurried into position. He handed Claude and Sir Bobblysock a list of jobs that needed to be done during the shoot.

The first thing was to hold
a long microphone on a
very long stick. It was
ever so heavy and
made Claude
wobble this
way and
that.

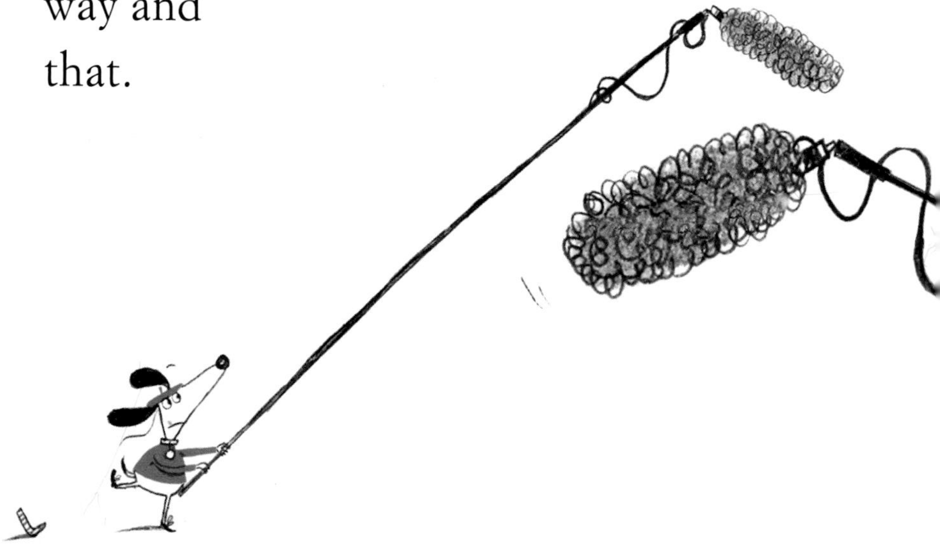

He came VERY close to
walloping a big piece of set.
Luckily, Sir Bobblysock was on
hand and a disaster was averted.

But all this meant that Claude
and Sir Bobblysock were too
busy to notice the washing line
start to snake its way out from
Claude's beret again...

The next job was to
swish a large spotlight
about so that it
followed Alan as
he swung down
Waggy Avenue.

Well, that was easier said than
done – the light was so heavy
Claude had to get Sir Bobblysock
to help, which he did.

Everard gave the two chums a
thumbs up.

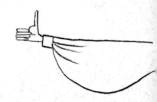

Sir Bobblysock suddenly
panicked. He thought he'd lost
one of his contact lenses on the
ground in all the excitement.
Claude swung the light around
for everyone to look for it. Then
Sir Bobblysock remembered that
he didn't actually wear contact
lenses – he'd just read about
someone who did in one of his
magazines and got confused.

All this kerfuffle meant that
no one noticed as a bit
more of the washing
line slipped out
and started to
dangle across
the floor...

Soon it was time for the big end scene to be recorded – the bit where Alan had to swipe Gloria Swoon away from Errol Heart-Throb just as he was giving her a big sloppy kiss, and then shimmy up the side of Miss Melon's shop.

Claude and Sir Bobblysock dashed
back to their seats so they could
get a good view of the action.

But, in all the rush, Claude didn't
see the washing line with all his
dressing-up costumes on it slip
out from his beret *completely*.

Claude also didn't see it get
tangled around some lights,
and some cameras, and around
Gloria Swoon and Errol Heart-
Throb's feet. Lastly, it knotted
around Everard Zoom-Lens and
his megaphone...

Claude only noticed when it was too late…

Errol Heart-Throb leant in to kiss Gloria Swoon. Just as Alan the gorilla started to drag her away to scamper up the building, the washing line pulled as tight as could be and…

THUD! CRASH! JANE

164

Lights and
cameras tumbled
everywhere! Everard
fell on his bottom, and
Gloria Swoon and
Errol Heart-Throb went
flying across the street...

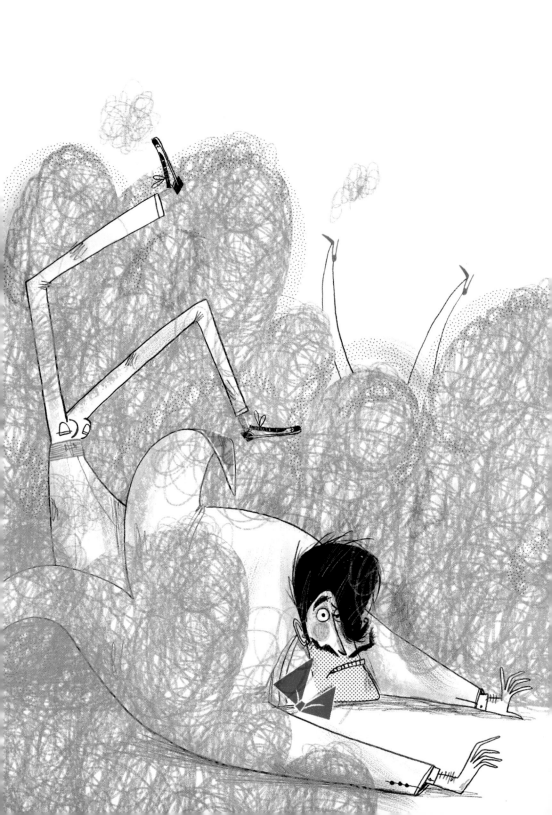

OOOOF!

'Uh oh...' said Claude.

Sir Bobblysock had one
of his hot flushes and
had to whip out his fan.

When the dust cleared, it became clear that all wasn't well.

Gloria and Errol had both twisted their ankles and had to go straight to the hospital.

As everyone dashed about to fix the mess, Everard Zoom-Lens let out a wail through his crumpled megaphone.

'Whatever will we do now?' he said. 'We can't make a film with our two lead actors in hospital! It's a disaster! If only we had two look-a-likes who could stand in for them.'

And he slumped down in a chair and went ever so limp.

Claude looked at his feet
and fiddled with the hem of
his sweater. He'd accidentally
caused this disaster with his
washing line full of dressing-up
clothes, and now he wanted to
fix it. But what could he do?

Then he had a STONKING idea!

'Me and Sir Bobblysock could
do it!'

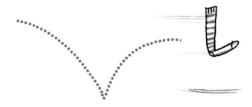

Everard smiled sadly. 'But you don't look a bit like Errol or Gloria...'

Claude smiled a hearty grin and reached into his beret.

'Just you wait!' he said.

The result was
MARVELLOUS!

'Goodness me!' cried Everard
Zoom-Lens. 'You look JUST
like Errol and Gloria – no one
will ever know the difference!
Extraordinary! Quick – let's get
the cameras rolling! ACTION!'

Well, what an afternoon
Claude and Sir Bobblysock had...

OH NO! I WILL SAVE YOU!

Claude shouted
his lines in his best
Outdoor Voice,
and he ran about
and lunged dramatically.

Sir Bobblysock turned out to be terribly
good at fluttering his eyelashes,
especially when Alan
the gorilla was
giving him the
collywobbles.

Miss Melons'

LOVELY PEAR
Fruit and Vegetable
Emporium

And when Claude bravely rescued Sir Bobblysock and carried him safely down the ladder to the ground, everyone clapped and hooted.

After Everard had shouted
'CUT!' he trotted over to
Claude and Sir Bobblysock,
grinning from ear-to-ear.

'You were STUPENDOUS!'
he said. 'Truly wonderful!
Won't you come with us
to Hollywood and be
famous movie stars?'

But before Claude
could answer, there
came an enormous
sob from somewhere
above their heads.

It was Alan.

He was standing on top
of the roof, crying and
fussing with his dicky bow.

'What's the
matter?'
cried Everard.

'I can't get
down,' said
Alan between
sobs.

'Use the
ladder!'
said Everard.

But Alan wouldn't.

If there was one thing he was
more frightened of than heights,
it was climbing down a ladder.

'Oh no!' said Miss Melons.
'I can't have my customers
choosing their cabbages and
picking their plums with a
gigantic gorilla crying all over
them!'

She was right, of course,
but Claude wondered if
he could help.

Was there some way
of getting Alan down
that was fun and not
frightening?

Of course there was!

'Come on, Alan!' cried Claude from his trampoline. 'This is a lot of fun!'

He carried on bouncing whilst Alan nervously shuffled closer to the edge.

Claude smiled his nice smile and even wagged his tail encouragingly.

182

At last, Alan covered his eyes,
took a deep breath and...

Miss Melons'

...leapt!

BOING!

184

BOING!

'A movie star AND a gorilla rescuer!' beamed Everard, joining Claude and Alan for a bounce. 'Are you sure you won't come and be a world famous actor?'

BOING!

Claude thought about it. He
certainly liked dressing up
and acting, but he also liked
pottering about at home. And
after the wigs, the sequins
and being manhandled by a
giant gorilla, Sir Bobblysock
desperately needed one of his
nice long lie-downs.

Claude explained all of this to
Everard Zoom-Lens. He was
disappointed, but understood.

'But you MUST keep all of the wigs!' he said, thrusting the box into Claude's paws. 'You did both look SO fetching in them.'

Claude and Sir Bobblysock thanked Everard Zoom-Lens, waved goodbye to all their new friends and went home.

Later that evening, when Mr and Mrs Shinyshoes returned home from work, they were jolly surprised not only to find a gorilla asleep in their kitchen, but to see that both he and Claude were wearing wigs.

'Do you think Claude knows anything about all this?' said Mrs Shinyshoes.

'Don't be silly!' said Mr Shinyshoes. 'Our Claude has been fast asleep all day...'

But Claude DID know
something about it.

And we do too,
don't we?

CLAUDE

Going for Gold

Claude is a dog.
Claude is a small dog.
Claude is a small, plump dog
who wears a lovely red jumper
and a very fetching beret.

very fetching
beret

lovely red
jumper

He lives at 112 Waggy Avenue
with Mr and Mrs Shinyshoes and
his best friend Sir Bobblysock.

This is Sir Bobblysock.

Every day, after Mr and Mrs Shinyshoes have cried, 'Toodle-pip, Claude!' and left for work, Claude and Sir Bobblysock go on an adventure.

Where will they go today?

It was a Tuesday and, for once, Sir Bobblysock couldn't wait to get out of the house.

Claude, you see, had woken up with ants in his pants. Not REAL ones, of course (that had been yesterday's excitement). He simply couldn't sit still!

He ate his breakfast with his bottom waggling about.

He brushed his teeth hopping on one leg.

And putting his beret on took
approximately 45 minutes because
he had to pretend that it was
first a pancake, and then a flying
saucer whizzing through space.
(A flying saucer that knocked
over two packets of cereal and an
entire jug of milk.)

Eventually, however, the two
chums made it out of the
front door.

Claude took a big sniff.

Today smelt of...

'ADVENTURE!' he said in his Outdoor Voice (because he was outdoors).

'LET'S GO AND FIND SOMETHING EXCITING TO DO!'

Sir Bobblysock was more interested in finding a frothy coffee and somewhere to park himself for a quiet moment, but he nodded his head in agreement.

And so the two friends bustled along Waggy Avenue.

Claude looked
for an adventure
everywhere.

Mr Lovelybuns was installing
a lovely big cream horn in his
front window, but that didn't get
Claude's eyebrows waggling this
morning. His tummy was still full
from breakfast.

200

Belinda Hintova-Tint had an appointment book FULL of curly perms to be done today, but that didn't get Claude's bottom wiggling. (Besides, Claude had helped her last week and Sir Bobblysock was still recovering.)

At Miss Melon's fruit and veg shop there was usually a funny-shaped cucumber or some plums that needed juggling, but today there was nothing.

Claude wandered back outside feeling deflated like a week-old balloon.

'There isn't an adventure to be found ANYWHERE!' he said to Sir Bobblysock and then immediately tripped up over his shoelaces and shot like a cannonball down the street.

202

203

Sir Bobblysock had ever such a job to keep up with him! It wasn't easy to clatter downhill and almost impossible whilst trying to balance a large frothy coffee and a handful of Garibaldis at the same time...

Eventually Claude came to a stop by walloping into a marching band who were right at that very moment **oomp-pah-pah-ing** around the corner with quite a crowd behind them.

When Claude managed to sit
up, his head was spinning.
Everyone was looking at him,
so Claude looked back at them.

What a strange group
they were!

JANGLE!

In amongst the band and the crowd of spectators waving flags were a lot of very healthy looking people. They appeared to be wearing JUST their vests and some very snazzy, stretchy knickers.

Sir Bobblysock whipped on his specs to get a better look.

Claude was about to ask what was
going on when a terribly hearty
woman in a leotard bounded over...

'GOODNESS!' she cried.
'I've never seen ANYONE
move so fast!'

Claude smoothed
down his ears.

'My name is Ivanna Hurlit-Farr,' she said, and she went on to explain exactly what on earth was happening.

Today was the day of the STONKING BIG SPORTS DAY where teams of people from all over the place were getting together to have a go at lots of sports. There would be medals for all the winners and a gigantic trophy too!

Ivanna wafted her hand in the
direction of two chaps holding
the most enormous glitzy gold
cup you have ever seen, as well
as a collection of little gold
discs on snazzy red ribbons.

'Oooooooooooh!'
went the crowd.

Claude had never seen anything so sparkly, and Sir Bobblysock was already thinking how lovely those medals would look around his neck. Especially if he wore them at the captain's table on a cruise or at a summer garden party.

'Can I join in please?' asked
Claude. This sounded like just
the sort of adventure he'd been
looking for!

Ivanna looked Claude up and
down. 'Do you have any sports
clothes? Any snazzy knickers?'

Well, Claude had a lot of things
in his beret, but he didn't think
he had any snazzy sports knickers.
He shook his head sadly.

'Never mind, I'm sure we can find you some!' said Ivanna encouragingly, lunging in her own.

Well, that sealed it! 'You're on the team,' cried Ivanna, 'and this must be your coach!'

She pointed at Sir Bobblysock who was still gazing at all the snazzy sports knickers and leotards around him.

Claude didn't like to say it was actually his best friend Sir Bobblysock, so he just nodded his head and the crowd shouted,

'HURRAH!'

Before they knew what was happening, Claude and Sir Bobblysock were up on Ivanna's shoulders and everyone cheered and ***oomp-pah-pahed*** their way to the STONKING BIG SPORTS DAY stadium.

It was only Sir Bobblysock
who noticed two people who
weren't cheering...

They were standing in the shadows
flipping coins and chewing on
toothpicks. Maybe they were on a
different team, he thought.

As the enormous gold cup and
the medals marched past,
they looked at each other and
chuckled to themselves in a
VERY naughty fashion.

Sir Bobblysock thought they too
were imagining how nice that
trophy would be on their knick-
knack shelf at home.

The STONKING
GREAT BIG
SPORTS DAY
stadium was
ENORMOUS.

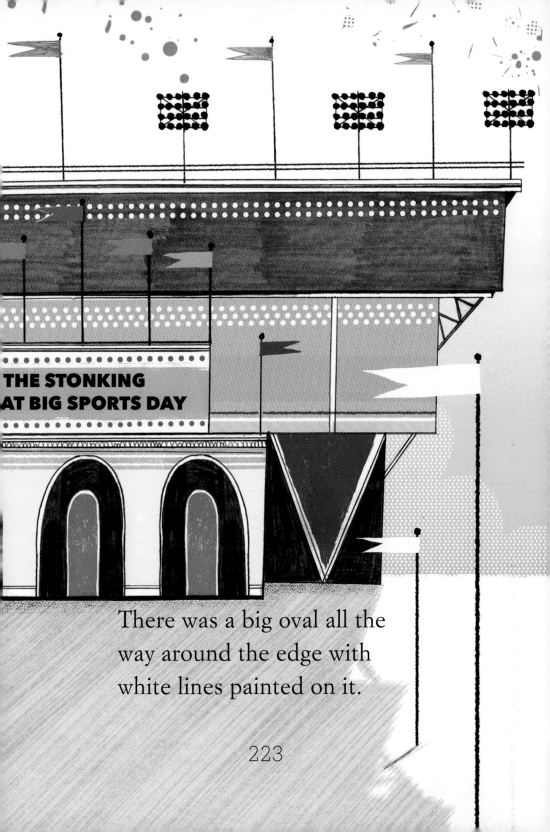

**THE STONKING
AT BIG SPORTS DAY**

There was a big oval all the
way around the edge with
white lines painted on it.

223

In the middle was a gigantic lawn that Claude thought could have done with a few flowers planted on it, or at least a nice water feature or something, to jazz it all up a bit.

There was also a big building with a 'Swimming Pool' sign on it, and various other rooms where different sports were played.

Claude helped place the trophy and medals on a special podium in the middle of the stadium and everyone clapped – it was going to be an exciting afternoon!

Whilst the crowd took their seats and the band popped their trombones away, Ivanna Hurlit-Farr eyeballed Claude. His jumper was lovely, but not quite the ticket for the day's events.

'Here are some sports knickers!' she said heartily. 'Do you have a vest you can wear with them?'

Well, of course, Claude did
– he always kept a vest in his
beret in case of sudden
draughts – so he wiggled into
that and put on the knickers.

They were gigantic!

'Oh dear…' said Ivanna.

'Don't worry!' cried Claude and he yanked them right up under his armpits. He wrapped the drawstring three times around his belly and finished it off with a nice bow.

Sir Bobblysock supervised from the side and told Claude that wearing his shorts like that would help to keep a chill off his kidneys.

Then Claude stashed his
beret down his vest and
popped on a sweatband.

Sir Bobblysock, wanting to get in the spirit of things now he was Claude's coach, put a whistle around his neck and popped a sweatband on too, even though he was dreadfully worried it would flatten his curly perm.

233

Gosh, did Claude and Sir
Bobblysock now look the part!

'LOVELY!' said Ivanna. 'Now
we are ready!'

Claude, Sir Bobblysock and all
their team mates cheered,
'HOORAY!'

The first event was Ivanna's favourite – the shot put.

What you had to do was hold a
ball, twirl around in a circle for a
moment or two, then hurl it as far
as you could across the lawn. Sir
Bobblysock thought it would make
a terrible mess of the grass, but
he didn't say anything.

Claude watched Ivanna and
the other competitors
throw the little ball
through the air.

236

'Now it's your turn, Claude!'
said Ivanna, and she handed
the ball to Claude.

It was terribly heavy. Claude
could hardly hold it. But he
tried his best and soon got in the
swing of twirling about in a circle.

Round and round and round
he went.

Sir Bobblysock had one of his
funny turns just watching him.

Then FLING! Claude let go
of the ball and...

FLING!

'OUC

...dropped it on Ivanna's toe!

Needless to say, their team did not win this competition.

240

'Don't worry!' groaned Ivanna, clutching her foot. 'Shot put is a bit tricky. Let's see how you do at running…'

The running competition was held on the big oval with the stripes painted on it.

Claude lined up with the other competitors. They seemed a jolly lot – even the two at the end of the line in the striped outfits and masks.

'When you hear a bang,' said Ivanna's team mate Reginald Hoofit, 'run as fast as you possibly can!'

Sir Bobblysock thought that it sounded exhausting and was worried Claude might get thirsty on the way round.

Suddenly he had a good idea –
he made Claude pour himself
a nice cup of tea from the flask
in his beret and gave him a
few Garibaldis. He told him to
make sure he had a good slurp
of tea and a biscuit as he ran to
keep his energy up.

245

Sir Bobblysock went to stand on the side with his earmuffs on as he didn't like loud bangs or the noise of squeaky plimsolls.

Claude got ready.

Claude got steady.

And when the bang went BANG!
Claude and all the other
competitors set off.

Claude ran as fast as he could.
His ears flew out behind him.
Sir Bobblysock was right –
running WAS thirsty work.
Thank goodness he had this
cup of tea…

He dunked a biscuit and
took a slurp and – OOPS!
– he found himself flying
through the air again…
He was out of control!
His tea and biscuits went
everywhere!

'WATCH OUT!' he cried through a mouthful of biscuit, but it was too late. He landed with a crash on Reginald and they went bouncing off the track and into the crowd.

CRASH

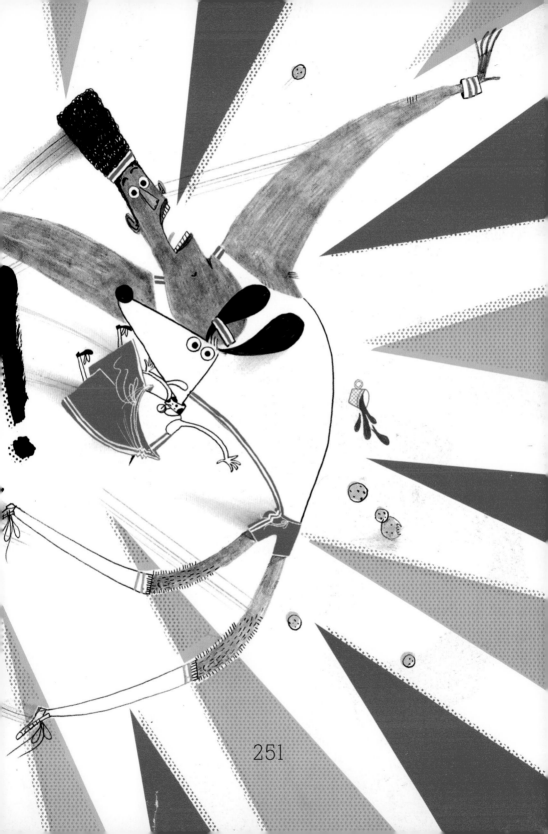

251

'Don't worry,' said Reginald a few minutes later as Ivanna put his arm in a sling, 'you might be better at something else…'

Sadly, that didn't seem to be the case.

Claude tried his best, but
nothing seemed to go right…

He and Sir Bobblysock spent
so much time blowing up his
armbands that Claude missed the
swimming competition entirely.

Then, he did a lovely gymnastics
routine, but when it came to
the bit where he had to waft
some ribbons about, Claude got
them tangled around his ears
AND around the chain of Sir
Bobblysock's spectacles, and
they both went CRASH! BANG!
WALLOP! straight into the
judges' table.

It was just disaster…
after disaster…

255

It turned out, however, that Sir Bobblysock was quite accomplished at synchronised swimming,

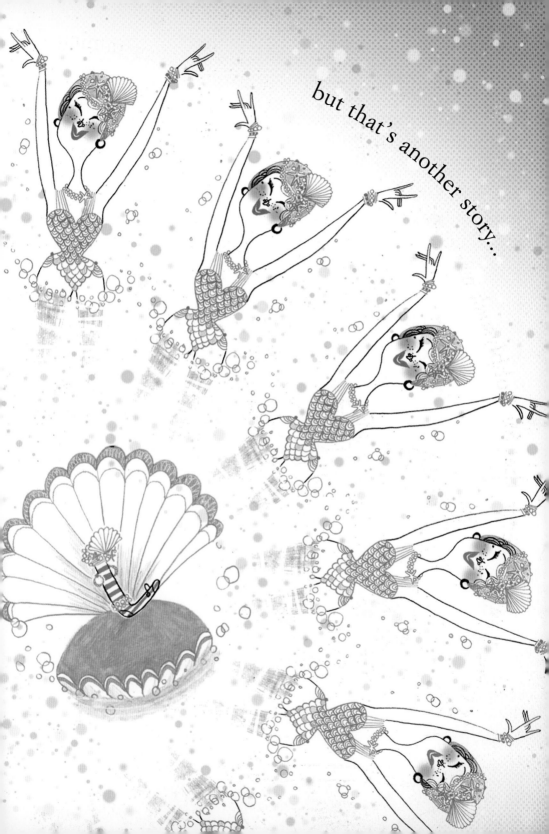

but that's another story...

'Never mind,' said Ivanna a bit sadly when everyone was taking a break, 'maybe we'll do better next year. And there's still the final event.'

Claude sat down next to Sir Bobblysock and swung his legs for a bit. Maybe he shouldn't join in the final event, he thought. Perhaps his team would do better without him. Maybe they'd even win some of those nice shiny medals.

Whilst Claude was thinking this, Sir Bobblysock was slathering himself in suncream and having a good nosy about the stadium.

All of a sudden he jumped!

'What is it, Sir Bobblysock?' said Claude. He followed Sir Bobblysock's gaze, and he was jolly glad he did too!

As he watched, the two people he'd spotted in striped outfits and masks earlier tiptoed sideways like crabs up to the podium with the trophy and medals on it. As quick as a wink, they grabbed them all and slung them into a useful sack that they'd had hidden all day down the leg of their sports knickers!

Sir Bobblysock had ALWAYS had a bad feeling about them.

'STOP!' cried Claude in his loudest Outdoor Voice, and started to run over to them. Sir Bobblysock quickly stashed his suncream into his gentleman's purse and followed. He didn't want to miss out on any of the action.

'WHAT ON EARTH DO YOU THINK YOU ARE DOING?'

cried Claude.

But the naughty robbers didn't stop to answer him – they scarpered!

And at exactly that moment the starting pistol went BANG! and the final event began!

Claude gave chase! Around the track he went, weaving in and out of the other runners. One of the other competitors (a very nice young man) picked Sir Bobblysock up so he could get a better view.

Claude chased them into the
cycling arena.

Claude stopped and rummaged
around his beret in his vest.

'Great blundering bone baguettes!'
he cried. He'd left his bike at home
today – just when he needed it!

With an eye on the now cycling robbers, Claude had another rummage around in his beret, found ONE of his roller skates and strapped it on.

WHOO

SH!

Around and around the arena he went, always almost, but not quite, catching the crooks… Then all of a sudden it was off the bike and onto the trampolines!

Then into the pool house – for the diving competition!

265

Claude waited patiently on the ladder for his turn behind the competitors and the thieves. He couldn't quite reach them!

'HAHAHA!' cried the crooks as they jumped off the high board. 'You'll never catch us!'

Claude clattered along the
board on his roller-skate and
peered over the edge.

Ooh! It was ever so high!

Sir Bobblysock, who was now
standing with the lifeguard,
started to tremble.

Claude gulped. If he didn't jump,
the robbers would get away!

Then he had an idea! Claude gave chase...

He **clanged** through the fencing hall,

hoofed it around the horse racing… and…

ping-ponged through some *very* tense table tennis matches.

But it was no good – he
just couldn't catch up with
the robbers. If they made it
around the track once more
they'd be able to run out of
the stadium and escape with
the trophy and medals!

Claude needed to beat them
to the finish line! But how?

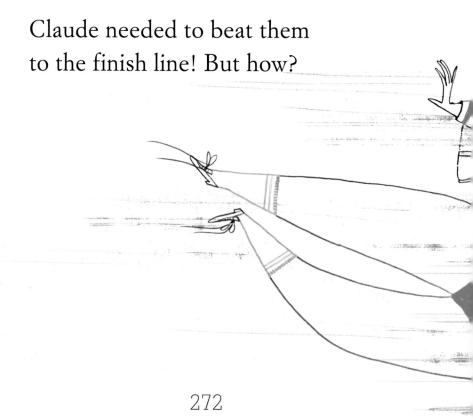

Then Sir Bobblysock had
the most wonderful idea. He
tooted his whistle and told
Ivanna all about it.

She rushed over to the
racing Claude and untied
his shoelaces with a flourish.
Claude immediately tripped
over them, just like earlier
        when he'd hurtled
            down Waggy
            Avenue!

273

Claude flew through the
air and landed straight
on top of the thieves!

The crowd went wild!

Ivanna, Reginald, Sir Bobblysock
and all the other competitors
hurried over to Claude.

'WELL DONE, CLAUDE AND SIR BOBBLYSOCK!' cried Ivanna. 'You caught these crooks, saved the trophy and medals AND won the final competition!'

The crowd whooped and hollered. Sir Bobblysock went quite dizzy with pride.

'Won't you stay and be a world famous sports superstar?' said Ivanna over the noise.

Claude thought about it for a moment. He'd had terrific fun having a go at all the sports, and he looked really quite dashing in his sports kit. But then he also really liked his nice cosy home on Waggy Avenue too.

He explained all this to Ivanna, and also that Sir Bobblysock needed to get back home so he could have a nice lie-down and sort out his hair which was going limp from all the excitement.

Ivanna said she understood and
then proudly presented Claude
with his special gold medals
and the huge, glitzy trophy. The
stadium went WILD!

Then everyone paraded Claude
and Sir Bobblysock home,
accompanied by the band who
played quite a jazzy medley.

Later on, when Mr and Mrs Shinyshoes came home, they were surprised to find a gigantic pair of sports knickers drip-drying on the radiator, and Claude tucked up in bed clutching an enormous trophy.

'Where on earth did it come from?' asked Mrs Shinyshoes. 'Do you think Claude knows something about this?'

Mr Shinyshoes chuckled. 'Of course not!' he laughed. 'He's been asleep here all day!'

But Claude DID know something about it, and we do too, don't we?

Phew! Claude has had quite a few adventures! You might be itching to set off exploring too after reading this book … Here are some top tips for a successful adventure from Claude himself!

Tip No.1:

You must be prepared for every eventuality. Bringing a beret full of potentially useful items is advisable.

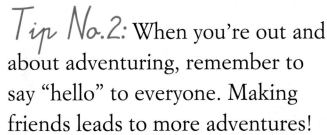

Tip No.2: When you're out and about adventuring, remember to say "hello" to everyone. Making friends leads to more adventures!

Tip No.3: Different adventures require different ensembles – make sure you're always dressed appropriately! You might need:

A snazzy BOBBLE HAT for a snowy adventure

WELLIES, if you plan to do some splishing and/or splashing

Some SPORTS KNICKERS for running-about-type adventures

Perhaps a WIG?!

(Sir Bobblysock thinks a HEAD TORCH might be more practical)

N.B. Always make sure you've combed your EARS!

Tip No.4: This is the most important tip – ALWAYS bring your very best friend along with you...!

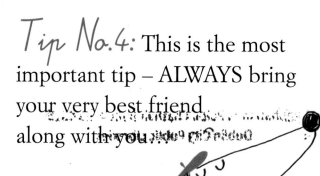

...that way you will have someone to share your memories with when you get back home!